DISTR

T0245904

HIT JUST RIGHT

Katherine Hengel

SADDLEBACK
EDUCATIONAL PUBLISHING

DISTRICT ⑬

SADDLEBACK
EDUCATIONAL PUBLISHING
www.sdlback.com

ISBN-13: 978-1-61651-584-3
ISBN-10: 1-61651-584-8
eBook: 978-1-61247-249-2

Printed in Malaysia

20 19 18 17 16   4 5 6 7 8

1

The large, black garbage bag was almost full. Carlos added a dustpan of popcorn. Then he tied off the bag. The theater was almost clean.

His best friend Esteban swept the last aisle. Esteban was telling a story about a pitching machine. Carlos didn't believe it.

"Get off it, Esteban!" Carlos laughed. "They're set at low speeds.

Only 50 miles per hour for Little League. That's not fast enough to kill a kid."

Esteban stopped sweeping. "Try 80 miles per hour," he said.

"Yeah, right! The pitches aren't that fast at the cages!" Carlos said.

"Look, it was unusual. *Very* unusual. But it did happen. One time," Esteban said. "I read it online. The kid turned too quick. His chest was wide open. The pitch hit him just right. Stopped his heart."

"That's what Jose needs," Carlos said.

"Forget that punk," Esteban said. "You'll show him this year, Carlos. I know it. All those hours at the cages? They'll pay off. You're twice the hitter he is. This year, you'll have no problems."

"I hope so," Carlos said. He wheeled the second garbage can toward Esteban. "If he starts with that 'Tubby' crap. I swear. I'll knock him out."

Esteban emptied his dustpan. "He won't," Esteban said. Then Carlos tied off the bag.

"Can you believe we start tomorrow? I can't wait to hit outside. On a real field," Carlos said.

"You tell Samson yet? That you're quitting the theater?" Esteban asked.

"No," Carlos admitted. "I was hoping you would. You know. Tell him for both of us."

"Don't you think you should? Tell him yourself?"

"I can't, Esteban. You're better at that stuff," Carlos said. "Come on. Please?"

Esteban exhaled. "Take these bags out to the alley. I'll tell Samson."

"Cool," Carlos said. "Meet me at the bus stop. I don't want to see Samson after."

Carlos pushed both garbage cans out the back. He was done! No more theater cleaning! The wheels were loud on the asphalt. Carlos lifted the first bag.

It had a leak. A nasty mixture of soda and butter dripped onto his pants. "Damn!" he yelled. He really hated working here. He only did it so he'd have money for the cages.

Carlos rolled the garbage cans back inside. He pushed them into the storage room. Then he ran to the bus stop. Esteban was already there.

"So? How'd he take it?" Carlos asked.

"Fine," Esteban replied. "No problem."

2

The next day, Carlos and Esteban went to school. They had study hall second period. It was in the library. They had to wait for a computer. As usual.

"What a joke," Esteban complained. "This school sucks. We need more computers."

Carlos nodded. But he wasn't worried about that. Practice started that night! The library windows were open. A cool breeze blew in. It would warm up later. Perfect for baseball!

All winter long, Carlos went to the cages. He never missed a Saturday. This year he would show up. He was a lot stronger now too. Last year he was soft and round. But this year, he was solid.

"Hey," Esteban said quickly. "Alicia is leaving. Let's get her computer."

Carlos grabbed his things. He followed Esteban. They stood by the row of computer desks. They had to let Alicia through.

Alicia moved slowly. She was wearing tight, black jeans and a tank top. Her black, lacy bra strap hung down her arm. She lifted it up as she passed them.

"Damn," Esteban said. "That girl *kills* me. She is so fine."

Carlos shook his head. She was too small for him. Plus, she was Jose's little sister. Trouble all the way around.

"Too skinny," Carlos said.

"You're crazy," Esteban replied.

Esteban sat in front of the computer. Carlos sat next to him. He leaned toward the screen. Esteban typed quickly. "What you looking for?" Carlos asked.

"A used phone," Esteban said. "Check it out. Not too bad. I could afford this!"

Carlos shrugged. "What about the monthly payment? How you gonna pay that? While you're playin' ball?"

Esteban stopped clicking. He rarely looked nervous. But he did now. He turned toward Carlos.

"What's up?" Carlos asked.

"I didn't quit last night, Carlos. At the theater. I just couldn't. I told Samson you were quitting. Just like I said I would. But I didn't quit."

Carlos leaned away from him. "What? Why?"

"I like having money, Carlos. A man's gotta earn. You feel me?"

"You're not playing *baseball* this year?"

"Carlos, you don't need *me*!" Esteban said. "All that practicing we did at the cages? You're a big hitter now!"

"What about Jose?"

"*Forget* Jose," Esteban said.

"Unbelievable," Carlos spat. "Thanks for punking out. All so you can buy crap."

Esteban looked hurt. "I have four sisters, Carlos. You're an only child. We got it harder than you. You don't get it."

Carlos was furious. "That phone for your sisters, Esteban? I don't think so," Carlos snapped. "Way to wait 'til the last minute to tell me. That's messed up, man."

3

The last bell rang. Carlos felt sick.
He wanted to skip practice. But he
couldn't. He'd worked too hard at
the cages. He could do this. With or
without Esteban.

Carlos walked to the field. Other
guys warmed up together. Carlos felt
so alone. He and Esteban were never
cool. But at least they had each
other.

Now Carlos had no one. He stood along the fence with his glove. He was sure Jose would tease him about being alone. Or maybe he'd call him Tubby again. Carlos wanted to walk off the field.

"Bring it in!" Coach yelled. "Let's start this season right. I expect respect. Respect each other and me. And keep your grades up. Now line up. Count off by fives."

The team did as Coach said. Carlos was a five. Luckily, Jose was a four. Coach sent each group to a station. Then he yelled, "Fives, come with me."

Carlos was happy to be a five. Fives got to hit first! He was still nervous. But in a good way now.

Coach led Carlos and the other fives. They did some warm-up exercises. Then they lined up to hit. Carlos went to the back of the line. Coach set up the pitching machine. Each player got five pitches.

Carlos saw Jose. His group was in the outfield. Jose looked ready for anything. He was a great outfielder. Very fast and skilled. "I get five chances," Carlos said to himself. "One of them will go long. I know it."

Soon it was Carlos's turn. He picked up a bat. It was the right weight. Other batters used the heaviest ones. But they couldn't handle them. Carlos knew the right bat for him.

"Ready?" Coach yelled.

Carlos nodded.

The pitching machine hurled the first pitch. It was just like at the cages! Carlos was comfortable. He lifted his left leg slightly. Then he turned his hips to the ball. He swung the bat. *Crack*!

It felt great! Good, clean contact. Carlos smiled. It sailed over the left fielder's head. Carlos brought the bat back into position. He was ready for his second pitch.

"Back it up," Jose yelled to the other outfielders. "Back it up I said!"

Carlos heard him. He felt so proud. He *was* a better hitter this year. Now even Jose knew it.

His next three hits were solid. But not as good as the first. Carlos had one pitch left. He would connect with that last one. He knew it.

And he did. The ball sailed straight down center field. Jose ran to the fence. Carlos watched. Would it clear the fence? Yes! Just barely. And just out of Jose's reach.

4

Carlos walked home after practice.
He was on top of the world. He hit
two balls over the fence! And Jose
didn't tease him. Not even once.

"How was practice, *niño*? My
boy?" his mother asked.

"Had some big hits, Mom!" Carlos
exclaimed. "A couple over the fence!"

"*Qué bien*! How wonderful!" his
mother replied.

Carlos' smile faded. "Esteban isn't playing this year."

"I figured," his mom said. "He called. Twice. He wants to know how it went."

Carlos thought about calling Esteban back. But he was still mad at him. He decided not to call. He'd talk to Esteban tomorrow.

The next day, Carlos walked to the library. It was time for study hall. That was usually a good thing. But not today. What would he say to Esteban? Did he want to talk to him?

Carlos walked in and sat down. He saw Esteban. He was at a computer, of course. His back was toward Carlos.

Five minutes passed. Carlos thought Esteban might apologize. He owed him that. Didn't he? Or should Carlos apologize for not calling him back?

Carlos knew Esteban's family was hard up. His mom often gave things to Esteban's family. Clothes. Dishes. Things like that.

It must be hard for Esteban. Carlos never really thought about it. Now he understood. He saw why money mattered to Esteban. He decided to forgive him. Forget waiting for Esteban to say he was sorry. Carlos missed his best friend.

Carlos walked toward him. But he stopped in his tracks. He saw Jose. He was walking up to Esteban.

"Hey. Give me that computer," Jose said.

"I just got here," Esteban said.

"I don't care. Give it to me."

"No."

The whole library heard it. Carlos froze. He wanted to help Esteban. But he was afraid of Jose. So he hid behind a row of books.

"Knock it off, Jose," Alicia said. "Just take mine." She stood up from her computer.

"Stay out of it, sis," Jose said. "I want *this* computer."

"I'm sure you do, Jose. But you're *not* getting it," Esteban said.

Their voices were loud. The library was quiet. So the librarian started walking over to them.

Jose stepped back. He pointed at Esteban. "You're on my list," he said to Esteban.

"Lucky me," Esteban replied.

Jose walked away. Carlos stayed hidden. Why should he stick up for Esteban? Esteban ditched him first. They'd each have to deal with Jose on their own now.

5

The next week flew by. Carlos and
Esteban talked at study hall. But
they didn't share a computer like
before. Something was different
between them now.

Carlos put all his energy into
baseball. The team was coming
together. Coach was happy with his
hitting. He even had him playing left
field!

Jose played center. It was awkward playing next to him.

Jose was such a good fielder. And so confident! He called for almost every ball.

Carlos was afraid to call for balls that came between them. He just let Jose catch them.

"Bring it in!" Coach yelled. "Good practice today," he said. "Everyone go home. Our first game is tomorrow. Get some rest tonight."

The team headed to the locker room. Coach called out to Carlos. "Got a sec?" he asked.

"Sure," Carlos said.

"You've improved, Carlos. I'm proud of you," Coach said. "Your hitting is excellent. You're doing good in the outfield too. But I'd like to see you go for more balls. Call for the ones you can get."

Carlos didn't know what to say. "Sure coach. I'll try."

Coach said, "Great. See you tomorrow. Now hit the showers."

When Carlos reached the school, Jose walked out. He was with a few guys from the team.

"Hey, Carlos," Jose said. "Busy tonight?"

Carlos was floored. He thought Jose was joking.

"Huh?"

"We're going to a movie. You in?"

"Um, sure."

"Good. Meet us outside the theater at 8:30."

6

"Later, Mom. I'm going to a movie,"
Carlos said.

"Okay," she replied. "Are you sure
though, Carlos? Shouldn't you rest
for tomorrow?"

"I'll be fine. I gotta go, Mom.
Hasta luego. See you later."

Carlos ran out the front door.
He had on his newest jeans, a black
T-shirt, and a baseball cap.

Carlos ran to the bus stop. It was like he was going to work. A week had passed since he quit. Well, since Esteban quit for him.

Carlos got to the theater. His heart raced. He saw the guys outside. He wondered if Esteban was working.

"What up, Carlos?" Anthony said. Anthony was their ace pitcher. Everyone said he'd get a scholarship. That's how good he was.

"Hey," Carlos said. "What movie we goin' to?"

"Main show is sold out," Jose said. "So we gotta see the one about a dumb king."

They walked into the theater. Carlos spotted Esteban right

away. He was working the popcorn machine.

Carlos bought his ticket. "I'm going to hit the bathroom," he told the guys. "Meet you in there."

Then Carlos snuck away. He walked along the edge of the lobby. He didn't want Esteban to see him. He just didn't.

Out front, Jose ordered popcorn. A large one. And a soda. Esteban set them on the counter.

"$5.75," Esteban said.

"Too much," Jose replied. "Try again."

"The price is $5.75," Esteban repeated.

Anthony overheard Jose. He rolled his eyes. "Give the kid a break,

Jose," he said. Anthony put six dollars on the counter. Esteban gave him the change.

"Enjoy the show," Esteban said.

"Oh, we will," Jose fired back.

But no one enjoyed the show. It was terrible! The theater was nearly empty at the start. Then one by one, folks left.

Anthony and the guys decided to leave too. "We're out of here," Anthony said. "See you tomorrow."

"See ya," Jose said. Then he put his hand on Carlos's arm.

"I need your help," Jose said to Carlos. He looked over his shoulder. He made sure Anthony and the guys were gone. It was just Carlos and Jose now.

"I'm sick of Esteban's mouth," Jose said. "Gonna teach him a lesson. Grab those sodas in the cup holders. Pour 'em on the floor."

Carlos froze. He couldn't.

"You chicken?"

"Jose, I can't …"

"Esteban disrespects me. This is what he gets. You gonna disrespect me too?"

Carlos shook his head. He felt weak in his knees. He grabbed a soda. There wasn't much in it. He poured in on the floor.

"Now the popcorn," Jose said. He walked each aisle. He took all the garbage people left. And he dumped it on the floor. Carlos did too. He just wanted it to be over.

That night, Carlos couldn't sleep. He thought about Esteban. Was he still cleaning? Was anyone helping him? Carlos almost threw up.

Backing out of baseball was one thing. Trashing the theater for no reason was another.

7

Carlos didn't sleep well. When he woke up, his eyes hurt.

"Ready for your game tonight?" his mom asked.

"I guess," Carlos said.

"*Estás bien?* You okay?" she asked.

"I'll be fine," Carlos said.

But he wasn't fine. How could he face Esteban?

Carlos saw him at study hall. He looked tired. "Must have worked all night," Carlos thought.

Carlos had never felt so horrible. He had to talk to Esteban. "Waiting for a computer?" Carlos asked.

"As always," Esteban said.

There was silence between them. Carlos wanted to say something. He almost asked Esteban how work was. Then he stopped himself.

Luckily, Esteban said something. "First game tonight. Right?"

Carlos was grateful. The silence was over. Esteban always was better at that kind of thing.

"Yep. First game. You comin'?"

"Of course," Esteban said. "Gotta see you hit one."

Carlos smiled. "You wanna hang out? After the game?" he asked.

Esteban frowned. "I don't know, man. Depends."

"On what?" Carlos asked.

"My date."

"Your *date*?" Carlos asked.

"You heard me. We might go out after. Maybe see a movie."

Carlos smiled. "Esteban! You got a lady now? Who is it?"

Esteban grinned. "You'll see," he said.

"Word," Carlos replied. "Try to catch a bit of the game. Okay? Don't miss it drooling over a girl."

Esteban laughed. "I'll be watching. Don't you worry."

8

Carlos warmed up with the team.
He stretched his arms and legs. He
took a swing in slow motion. Then at
half speed. Then at full speed. He did
every warm-up he ever learned.

Coach could tell he was nervous.
"Carlos. Relax out there. All right?"

Carlos nodded.

"You're at home, kid. Look at all
those fans!" Coach said.

Carlos looked up in the stands. Coach was right. A lot of fans showed up. But where was Esteban? Carlos scanned the crowd. It took a minute to find him.

Esteban was carrying sodas and hot dogs. He moved slowly through the stands. Finally he made it to his seat. It was right next to Alicia!

Carlos smiled. Esteban had the girl of his dreams! He'd just spent a fortune on her too. Carlos watched Esteban pass the food to Alicia. They both looked happy. "A man's gotta earn," he thought.

The band played the national anthem. Carlos's stomach started rolling. He wasn't feeling calm. Not at all.

Carlos' team took the field. He ran out to left field. Jose went to center.

The first batter hit a deep fly ball. Deep to left-center. Jose called it. But Carlos should have. It was closer to him.

Jose made a big dive. He rolled several times. When he stopped, he held up the ball.

The crowd went wild. But Carlos felt bad. At the end of the inning, he jogged to the dugout. Coach didn't say anything. But Carlos knew what he was thinking.

It was the bottom of the second. There was still no score. Carlos got his first at bat. He struck out to end the inning.

"Where's your bat tonight?" Jose asked. Carlos wanted to ask him the same thing. Jose made an out too. But he didn't say anything.

Carlos batted again in the fourth and sixth innings. He hit it pretty deep both times. But they were both caught.

Soon it was the seventh and final inning. The score was tied.

Carlos grabbed his glove. He stood up. "Call the balls that are yours, Carlos," Coach said. "You know which ones they are. You can do it. Now get out there."

Anthony pitched well in the seventh. He struck out two batters. But then two runners got hits. They were on first and third.

The next batter hit one deep. It was the leadoff hitter. He hit it to the same spot. Just like the first inning.

This time Carlos called the ball right away. But that didn't stop Jose. He kept coming.

Carlos tried to watch the ball. But he had to watch Jose too. They both went for the catch. They hit each other. The ball fell to the grass.

Jose quickly picked it up. He threw the ball home. But it was too late. Both runners scored.

Anthony struck the next batter out. The top of the seventh was finally over. But the other team was ahead by two runs.

Carlos ran to the dugout. Coach did not look happy. "Who called that ball?" he asked. Neither Jose nor Carlos spoke.

"Well?" Coach said. "No one even *called* it?"

"I called it," Jose blurted out. Carlos's jaw dropped.

Coach looked at Carlos. "That true, Carlos?" Coach asked.

Carlos couldn't speak. He wanted to tell the truth. But he couldn't.

"It's true," Carlos said quietly.

"What's that?" Coach asked.

"I said Jose called it," Carlos said. Then he walked to the end of the bench. He didn't bat again. His team went down in order in the bottom of the seventh. The game was over.

9

Coach called the team together.

"We did a lot of things right," he said. "Anthony pitched a great game. Carlos hit the ball hard a couple of times. They would have been out of a lot of parks. Just not this one."

Carlos couldn't look up. He kept his head down.

"We also did some things wrong," Coach said. "The infield made some mistakes. That missed double-play in the third. It might have changed the game. We also had some errors in the outfield."

"Because Jose's a ball hog," someone said. Carlos looked up. Who said that? And why wasn't Jose all over it?

"Where the hell *is* Jose?" Coach asked. He looked around the huddle.

"He left, Coach," Anthony said.

"Where'd he go?"

"Don't know, Coach," Anthony replied.

"Unacceptable. He'll pay for that at practice. Mark my words. We don't need that crap. We need teamwork. We got two games next week. Let's do better than today. Bring it in."

Everyone put a hand in the middle of the huddle. "Team, on three. One, two, three, *team!*"

Carlos and Anthony picked up the bats. The rest of the team went inside. "You called that ball. Didn't you?" Anthony said.

Carlos kept his head down. "I don't know," he said.

"Stop lying, Carlos. I heard you call it. You gotta stand up to him."

"I know," Carlos said.

Anthony grabbed one bat bag. Carlos grabbed the other. They headed to the school.

"Coach is gonna ride Jose at practice," Anthony said.

"Why did he leave?" Carlos asked. "Right after the game?"

"Didn't you see Alicia? In the stands with Esteban?"

Carlos stopped walking. Of course. Jose hated Esteban! No way he wanted him with his sister.

"I love that kid," Anthony continued. "I wish he'd come back on the team. He's small. But he ain't scared. Remember when he—"

"I have to go," Carlos interrupted. He dropped the bat bag. "Anthony, can you take this?"

"I got it, Carlos. Go do what you gotta do."

10

Carlos took the bus to the theater.
He ran to the ticket counter.

"Hey, Juan," Carlos said. "Did
Esteban come in tonight?"

"He sure did! He was with a little
hottie too."

"What movie did they catch?"
Carlos asked.

"Uh, the 9:15," Juan said. "It's
almost over. They'll be out in ten

minutes. Think he's gettin' some in there, Carlos?"

"I hope so," Carlos said. "Tell him I'm outside?"

"No problem," Juan said.

Carlos left the theater. He didn't know what to do. He looked across the parking lot. It was full.

Then he saw Jose. He was leaning against the bus shelter. It was at the far edge of the lot.

Carlos took a deep breath. He started walking towards Jose.

"Did Coach send you, Carlos?" Jose sneered. "'Cause I missed his little pep talk?"

Carlos didn't say anything.

"Not Coach, huh? I know! You're here to save Esteban! Am I right?"

Still, Carlos didn't say a thing.

"Come on, Carlos," Jose teased. "You won't do anything. We both know that."

Carlos could feel his heart racing. He felt like he was on fire.

"Go home," Jose said. "You don't want to see this. Trust me. Here comes the little punk now."

Carlos turned. He saw Esteban crossing the lot. Alicia was with him.

"How was your date?" Jose yelled.

"None of your business," Esteban said.

Jose kept talking. "Me and Carlos. We had a date too. Last night. Right, Carlos? Carlos got a little wild. Trashed the theater! Said he always hated the place!"

Esteban didn't believe it. "That'd never happen," he said.

"Ask him!" Jose yelled.

Esteban looked at Carlos. Carlos lowered his head. "It's true," he whispered.

"Bet that burns. Huh, Esteban? Bet you wanna do *this*."

Jose grabbed the front of Carlos's shirt. He pushed him hard. Carlos fell backwards.

"Don't date my sister, Esteban. I'll take you apart," Jose said. He walked toward Esteban.

Alicia got between them. "I'll do what I want, Jose! Stay out of it!" she shouted.

Carlos got up. He ran at Jose. He shoved him against the bus shelter.

With his left hand, Carlos held Jose against the shelter. He brought his right fist back. He slammed it into Jose's jaw.

Jose slid to the ground. Esteban and Alicia were stunned. Carlos was too. They all stared down at Jose.

A bus stopped at the shelter. "That's your bus, Jose," Esteban said.

Jose slowly stood up. He walked to the bus. Then he stopped at the door. "You're on my—" Jose said.

"List," Alicia said. "We know. Just go home, Jose." The bus door closed. Jose was gone.

Carlos sat on the bus bench. He looked at his right hand. It was bruised. "I've never hit anyone before," he said.

"You sure?" Esteban asked. "Looked pretty pro to me."

Carlos looked at the ground. His shoulders sank.

"Esteban, about the theater. I'm sorry, man," he said. He looked up at Esteban. "What can I do? To make it right? Anything. You name it."

Esteban smiled. He put his fists up. Then moved his head from side to side.

"Teach me your moves!" he said. He slapped Carlos's shoulder. "You dropped that fool, Carlos! Looked like a pitching machine hit him."

Carlos smiled. "Best hit I had all night."